For my mother and father,
Louisa and Raymond Young,
with love and thanks

With grateful acknowledgment to: Joy Peskin and the team at FSG; my
agent, Linda Pratt; Paul Merewether for all he does and is; work buddies
Laurie Keller, Margaret Willey, and Sue Stauffacher; and special skills / life
mentors James Kelly, Antoin Mac Gabhann, and Lucy Steinlage.

Farrar Straus Giroux Books for Young Readers
175 Fifth Avenue, New York 10010

Copyright © 2016 by Amy Young
All rights reserved
Color separations by Bright Arts (H.K.) Ltd.
Printed in China by Toppan Leefung Printing Ltd.,
Dongguan City, Guangdong Province
Designed by Kristie Radwilowicz
First edition, 2016
5 7 9 10 8 6 4

mackids.com

Library of Congress Cataloging-in-Publication Data
Names: Young, Amy, author, illustrator.
Title: A unicorn named Sparkle / Amy Young.
Description: First edition. | New York : Farrar Straus Giroux, 2016. |
Summary: A picture book about a little girl who desperately wants a beautiful unicorn as a pet,
but winds up with a little less than desirable one instead—Provided by publisher.
Identifiers: LCCN 2015036849 | ISBN 9780374301859 (hardback)
Subjects: | CYAC: Unicorns—Fiction. | Goats—Fictions. | Pets—Fiction. | BISAC: JUVENILE
FICTION / Animals / Mythical. | JUVENILE FICTION / Animals / Pets. | JUVENILE FICTION /
Social Issues / Friendship.
Classification: LCC PZ7.Y845 Un 2016 | DDC [E]—dc23
LC record available at http://lccn.loc.gov/2015036849

Our books may be purchased in bulk for promotional, educational, or business use. Please
contact your local bookseller or the Macmillan Corporate and Premium Sales Department at
(800) 221-7945 ext. 5442 or by e-mail at MacmillanSpecialMarkets@macmillan.com.

A Unicorn Named SPARKLE

Amy Young

FARRAR STRAUS GIROUX

NEW YORK

The ad said "Unicorn, 25 cents."

Lucy sent in the money.
She could hardly wait.

"I will name him Sparkle. He will be blue
with a pink tail and a pink mane."

A whole day passed.

"I will put flowers around his neck.
He will let me ride on his back."

Another day passed.

"I will take him to show-and-tell. Everyone will love him."

"He might be scared when he first gets here.
I will give him a cupcake."

"Sparkle, Sparkle, where are you?"

Finally a big truck rumbled up. It was the unicorn man!
He left a large box on the porch.

"It's Sparkle!"

Lucy opened the box carefully, gently.

"CHOMP!"

The cupcake was gone.

"Sparkle, come back!"

"Sparkle, not
the underpants!"

"NO!"

He was not what she expected. He had spots.
His ears were too long. He smelled funny.

Oh, and he had fleas.

Lucy put a flower
necklace on him.

He ate it.

She put a
tutu on him.

He ate that, too.

He did not want to be ridden.
He bucked her right off.

He did not want

to go

to show-and-tell . . .

Lucy was mad.
"You are a bad unicorn."

She walked away.

Sparkle followed her.

Stop that!

Lucy called the unicorn man.
"Take him back. I don't want him."

"Okay, but I can't get there until tomorrow."
Lucy could hardly wait.

That night there was a storm. Sparkle was afraid.
Lucy gave him Bear-Bear so he would stop pestering
her. It wasn't enough. She had to read him a bedtime
story, too, and give him warm milk to drink.

He licked her hand. She patted his head and said,
"Don't be such a big baby." His fur was very soft.

At last he fell asleep.

The next morning, Lucy watched Sparkle
play in the yard. He liked the butterflies,
and they liked him.

Some boys came by and asked,
"What's your goat's name?"

"His name is Sparkle, and he is not a goat."

"He looks like a goat."

"Well, he is not a goat. He is a special
kind of unicorn."

After the boys left,
Lucy watched Sparkle
play some more.

She had to admit: sometimes he made her smile and sometimes he made her laugh.

The unicorn man drove up.

Okay, let's load him in.

Sparkle did not want to get into the box.

Lucy put a cupcake in the far corner. Sparkle loved cupcakes, so he went in.

Lucy shut the door. Sparkle asked,

"B-E-E-E-H?"

The unicorn man revved his engine
and drove away.

Lucy yelled,

WAAAAIT!

Sparkle bleated,

BAAAH!!

The truck stopped. Lucy opened the box
and Sparkle jumped out. He was so excited
that he knocked her down by mistake.

"SPARKLE," said Lucy.

"Welcome home!"